The Secret of
THE RED SHOES

A STORY ABOUT AN ELDERLY GREAT-GRANDMOTHER

BY JOAN DONALDSON
ILLUSTRATED BY DORIS ETTLINGER

gpKids™

Nashville, Tennessee

ISBN 0-8249-5522-6

Published by GPKids
An imprint of Ideals Publications
535 Metroplex Drive, Suite 250
Nashville, Tennessee 37211
www.idealsbooks.com

Color separations by Precision Color Graphics, Franklin, Wisconsin

Printed and bound in Italy by LEGO

Library of Congress Cataloging-in-Publication Data

Donaldson, Joan.
   The secret of the red shoes / by Joan Donaldson ; illustrated by Doris
Ettlinger.
      p. cm.
   Summary: Great-grandma's secret makes for a wonderful surprise at
the party celebrating her one hundredth birthday.
   ISBN 0-8249-5522-6 (alk. paper)
   [1. Great-grandmothers—Fiction. 2. Shoes—Fiction. 3. Parties—
Fiction.]   I. Ettlinger, Doris, ill. II. Title.
PZ7.D714985Sec 2005
[E]—dc22
                                        2005014642

10 9 8 7 6 5 4 3 2 1

Designed by Eve DeGrie

For Margo, Alexis, Abigail, and Grandma Bunny, who all wore
red shoes at Great-Gramma Coburn's 100th birthday party.
May your red shoes always sing.
—J.D.

To the gifted staff of Warren Haven,
Oxford, New Jersey. And thank you to my models, Finita Fensel and Sloan Dowd.
—D.E.

To the Parents
By Vicki Wiley

Children who live with an elderly person often don't understand or appreciate the older person. But children may have a high regard for the elderly in spite of frustrations with their physical limitations.

When asked to describe an older friend or relative, a child will often use words like "friendly," "wonderful," and "good." Children between the ages of two and seven years also mention the physical attributes that they actually see: gray hair, a cane, perhaps a walker or wheelchair. Children of all ages often recognize hearing or memory impairment.

The potential benefits of a relationship between a child and an elderly person, however, are so great that caring adults can help the child see beyond differences of age.

A great way to connect the generations is through storytelling. Children love stories, and the elderly always have a story to tell! In this way the elderly person can also pass down a priceless legacy of beliefs and experiences.

Some relationship-building topics to suggest include:

*Do you remember a time when your faith changed your life?

*What has been the most difficult time of your life? How did you get through that time?

*Was there an event that changed the course of your life?

*How did you and Grandma (or Grandpa) meet?

Remember to let the child tell his or her stories too. Through storytelling, members of each generation gain insight into the lives of the other, and both will grow in understanding of and love for one another.

Vicki Wiley holds a Master of Arts in Theology, with an emphasis on children in crisis, from Fuller Seminary. At present, she is Director of Children's Ministries at First Presbyterian Church in Honolulu, Hawaii.

I was the only one who knew Great-Grandma's secret.

When she visited, she played dolls with me. Great-Grandma picked out a pair of red shoes and stuck them on her fingers. She tiptoed the slippers across the table.

"I've never told anyone this," Great-Grandma said, "but I've always wanted a pair of red shoes. When I was in third grade, I went to a Christmas party. Eliza Jean wore red shoes that sparkled like dew-covered strawberries. I wanted red shoes that sparkled too.

"When my daddy took me to town, I'd stare at the red shoes in the store windows. But he only bought me high-top shoes, sometimes black, sometimes brown.

"I'd lace them over the thick stockings my mama knit. The high-tops kept my feet dry when I walked along the creek and through the orchard to school, but those boots couldn't sing like red shoes."

"Shoes can't sing!" I looked at my purple sandals. I'd never heard them sing.

Great-Grandma answered, "Red shoes can, if you listen hard enough." She set down the doll shoes.

"After I finished school, I married your great-grandpa and took to wearing ankle socks and oxfords. I'd balance a baby on my hip while I drove the team, and your great-grandpa John loaded the hay. I felt safe with those clunkers on. They were sturdy shoes, but they couldn't skip like red shoes."

"Your shoes skipped?" I asked her.

"As fast as the wind," Great-Grandma said, as she leaned back in her chair. "Now for church, I wore narrow black shoes that I slipped on over silk stockings. Those Sunday shoes lasted years. They squeezed my toes and kept them quiet while the preacher prayed, but they couldn't dance like red shoes."

"I have pink ballet slippers." I kicked off my sandals and put the ballet slippers on. "See! They make my feet dance."

Great-Grandma smiled. "Yes, such happy feet. I never had the money for ballet slippers like yours, but I've lived a blessed life. God always gave us what we needed."

She nodded at her slippers. "Now I mostly wear these old things. No bows or buckles, but they keep my toes toasty." She stood and yawned. "Time for my nap, Abby."

Great-Grandma shuffled off to the guest bedroom. I studied my sandals. When I pumped the swings in the park, the wind swooshed through my toes. Was that how shoes sang?

Later, Mama sat at the kitchen table planning a birthday party for Great-Grandma.

"Can I make the invitations now?" I asked. "You said I could."

"Yes. Why don't you color while Great-Grandma sleeps?"

"I'll draw a hundred balloons. One for each year." I spread out my crayons.

"I wish we could do something special for her." Mama tapped her pencil.

I looked at the pile of shoes by the back door. I'd never heard any of them sing.

"Mama!" I leaned over and whispered the secret in her ear.

Mama laughed and picked up the phone. She told all her brothers and sisters. Everyone went shopping.

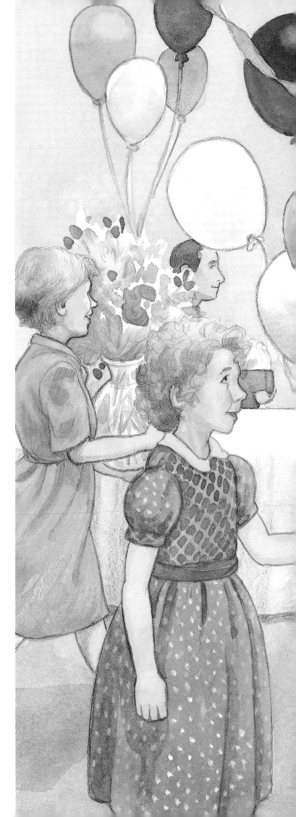

My whole family giggled as we
drove to the hall for the party.
   We decorated the big room with
balloons and streamers.

Finally, Great-Grandma arrived,
holding Daddy's arm.
I handed Great-Grandma the
fancy-wrapped present.

When Great-Grandma opened
the box, her eyes shone like
stars. She picked up the red
shoes, those shiny shoes with
buckles and bows that knew
how to skip and dance. Her
mouth made a little O.

I held up my foot. Mama
lifted hers. Great-Grandma stared
at our feet. She started to cry.

Everyone wore red shoes. The dads and boys
had new high-top sneakers. Mama and her sisters
waltzed in satin pumps.

My big sister and cousins swished their skirts
above high heels. And I skipped circles around
them in my red Mary Janes.

When we gathered around
Great-Grandma to have our picture
taken, even our feet smiled.

I squeezed Great-Grandma's hand.
She whispered, "Thank you."

Our shoes sparkled in the light of
a hundred candles.

And I could hear those red shoes sing.

In Their Own Words

Joan Donaldson

I grew up in Michigan and my parents bought me red sandals that skipped through my summers, but *The Secret of the Red Shoes* danced into my imagination when my lifelong friend, Margo, described her grandmother's one-hundredth-birthday celebration. Margo's extended family had surprised Mrs. Coburn with her first pair of red shoes, and everyone at the party wore red shoes. Because Mrs. Coburn grew up in rural Wisconsin in the early 1900s, she experienced a more simple childhood than her great-grandchildren, as shown through Abby's dialogue. But the love of family resides in the heart of both.

I still stomp around my organic blueberry farm near Lake Michigan in red rubber clogs; and when my two sons lived at home, they helped on the farm in their work boots. Whatever color of shoe you slip onto your feet, I hope you can hear them sing! —J.D.

Doris Ettlinger

I spent many precious hours listening to my Nana tell fairy-tale-like stories of her childhood in a village on the edge of the Black Forest in Germany. I know that someday a small boy or girl will sit beside my children, Ivy and Ben, and listen as they describe growing up in a never-completely-fixed-up gristmill on the edge of the Musconetcong River in New Jersey. May the stories continue. —D.E.